umpelstiltskin's Child

written and illustrated by

Bonnie Ferrante

For Kathy Balec,
the kindest friend a person could have.

ISBN 978-1-928064-12-1
ALL RIGHTS RESERVED
Single Drop Publishing
Second Edition
Copyright 2014

**E**ven though he could spin straw into gold, Rumpelstiltskin felt as gloomy as rain on a festival day. Spinning gold gave him horrible headaches. No one seemed to care.

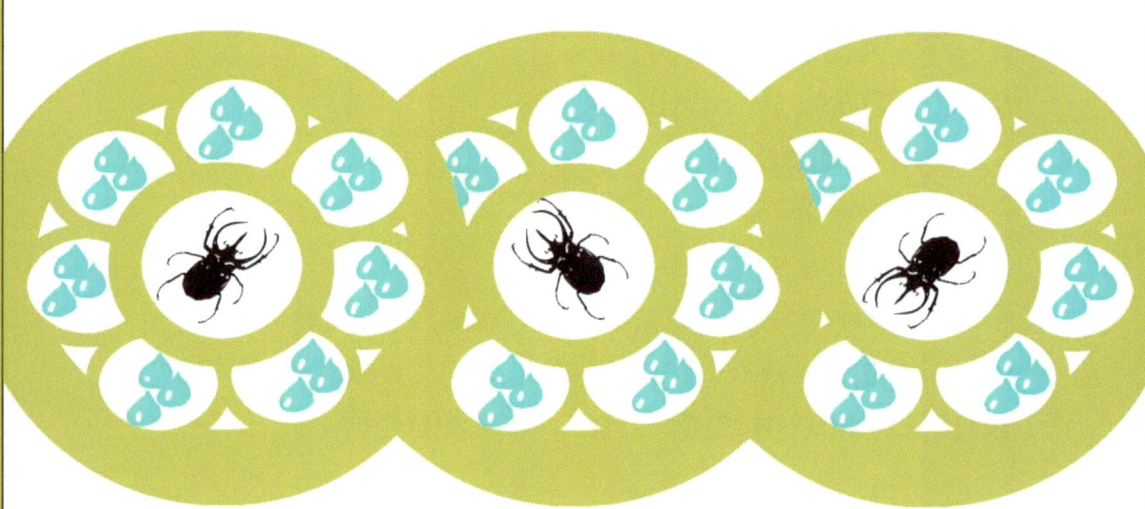

No one ever asked about his garden or fishing or even how he was. Rumpelstiltskin felt as unwanted as a bug in the soup.

ver and over, the villagers pressured him to spin more straw into gold.

"Fill my cup with gold," said the tinsmith's wife, "so I can buy a new dress."

Rumpelstiltskin hid whenever he saw a villager coming. Sometimes he stamped his foot and disappeared.

"y head hurts too much," Rumpelstiltskin said. "I'm only going to spin straw into gold when I really need it."

"If that odd little man won't spin gold for us, what good is he?" said a villager. "He's such a fool."

The children were the only ones who met him with smiles. Rumpelstiltskin gave them bread with honey, fresh peas from his garden, and crunchy homemade pickles.

"Don't come here anymore," said the baker. "The only thing I want you to bring my children is gold."

 t broke Rumpelstiltskin's heart to be shunned by the villagers. He stopped shaving, cutting his hair, and even bathing. People called him the dirty little hermit.

As he fished from the river bank one afternoon, Rumpelstiltskin saw a boy lean over the water, wobble, and fall. Rumpelstiltskin threw down his rod and jumped in.

he water was cold as midnight and fierce as a swarm of hornets. Rumpelstiltskin pulled the child to shore. He carried the small body into town.

The villagers shouted, "Monster!"

Rumpelstiltskin gently set the child on the grass and ran home.

WANTED

Frightened for his life, Rumpelstiltskin packed his possessions and disappeared, forgetting his fishing rod on the river bank. He did not stop until he was far, far away from the village.

 he next day, as he passed a stone building with a locked door, he heard a young woman crying, "Please, please, can't someone help me?"

Using his magic, Rumpelstiltskin popped inside.

"What's wrong?" he asked.

"My mother told the prince I could spin straw into gold. If I don't change this pile of straw, he will leave me here to starve.

But, if I do change it, he'll marry me and I'll never be hungry again."

Rumpelstiltskin smiled. "I could spin the straw into gold for you, but my price is high."

"When I am a princess, I can give you anything you want," said the woman.

Rumpelstiltskin spun the straw into gold as she slept. In the morning, he said, "I want your first born child."

he woman married the prince and had a son. When Rumpelstiltskin came, the princess sobbed. "How can you take a baby away from his mother?"

Rumpelstiltskin felt a lump in his throat. "If you can guess my name within three days, I will let you keep the baby."

he princess sent her men out to find all the unusual names they could. On the first night, she guessed.....

"No, none of those," said Rumpelstiltskin.

On the second night she guessed...

"No, not even close," said Rumpelstiltskin.

The princess wiped her eyes.

On the third night, the princess's personal guard saw a campfire in the King's forest. He slowly crept up in the dark and spotted a small man dancing around the fire and chanting.

"The princess will never win this game.
Rumpelstiltskin is my name.
I will have her little boy
He will fill my life with joy."

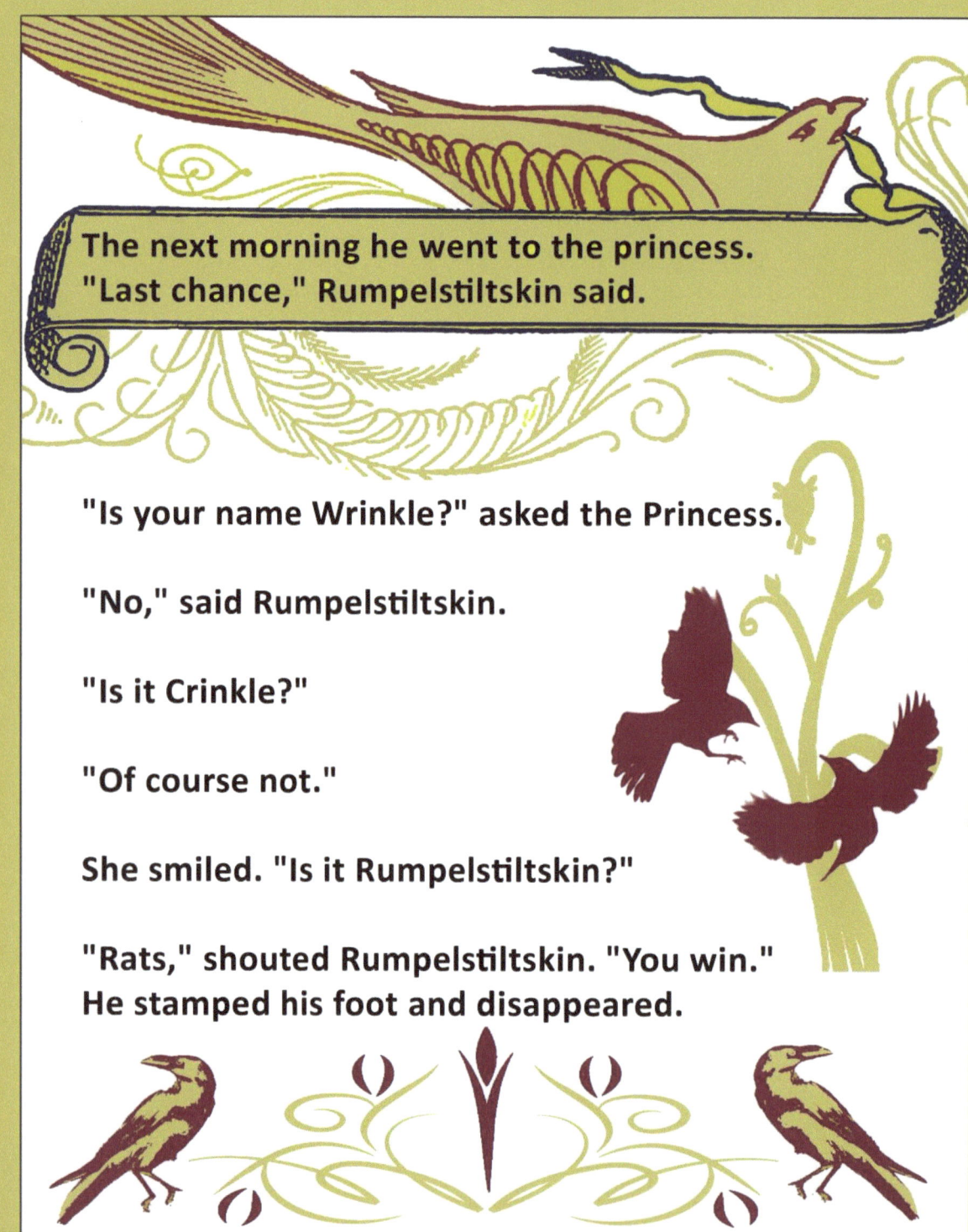

The next morning he went to the princess. "Last chance," Rumpelstiltskin said.

"Is your name Wrinkle?" asked the Princess.

"No," said Rumpelstiltskin.

"Is it Crinkle?"

"Of course not."

She smiled. "Is it Rumpelstiltskin?"

"Rats," shouted Rumpelstiltskin. "You win." He stamped his foot and disappeared.

So there he sat, by his campfire, no village, no friends, no family, and no baby. He was as lonely as the last tomato on the vine. As the logs burned down to glowing coals, Rumpelstiltskin decided it was time to go home. First he shaved, cut his hair, and had a bath.

29

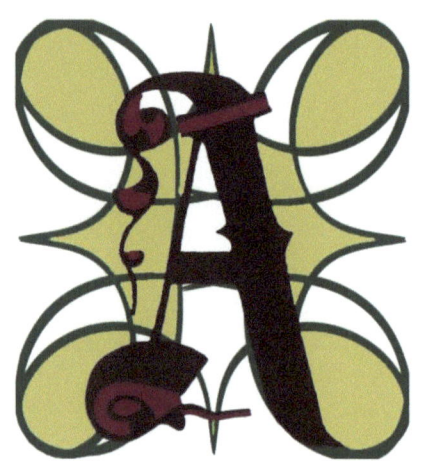

s Rumpelstiltskin entered the village, the smith stopped hammering his iron. The cobbler stopped sewing his leather. The tanner stopped scraping his hide.

When Rumpelstiltskin reached the middle of town, the villagers silently approached.

The mason pointed. "You're back."

Rumpelstiltskin's heart thumped like a trout tossed on shore.

"We've been looking for you," said the baker.

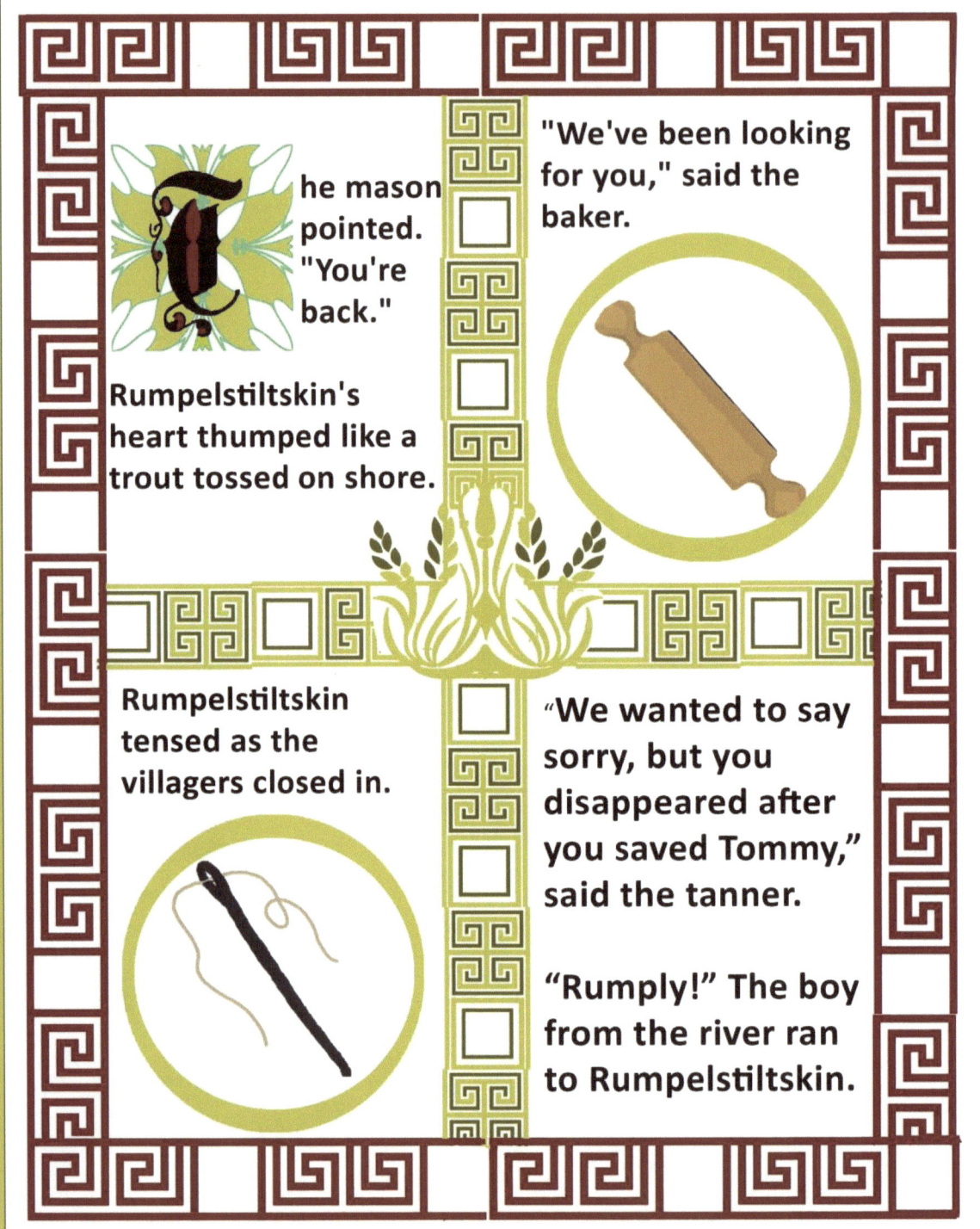

Rumpelstiltskin tensed as the villagers closed in.

"We wanted to say sorry, but you disappeared after you saved Tommy," said the tanner.

"Rumply!" The boy from the river ran to Rumpelstiltskin.

"ommy's an orphan." said the tailor who wore his needle in his feathered hat, "but I have seven children of my own."

"Why don't you take him?" askedthe cooper.

Rumpelstiltskin stood taller. "I'd love to be Tommy's family."

Rumply was loved by the villagers for his kindness and generosity. Whenever a child was orphaned, he added another room to his home. It was always filled with the sound of laughter and Rumply laughed most of all.

When the princess's child turned eighteen, Rumpelstiltskin sent him a gold ring. It had a large emerald set between two bundles of straw. On the card he wrote, "Happy Birthday. From Guess Who."

THE END

Discussion Questions

1. The villagers stopped being friendly with Rumpelstiltskin when he wouldn't spin gold. Was this fair?

2. Why did Rumpelstiltskin jump into the river to save Tommy?

3. When Rumpelstiltskin rescued Tommy from the river, the villagers assumed the worst. Why?

4. Do you think Rumpelstiltskin should have taken the Queen's baby?

5. Why do you think Rumpelstiltskin gave the Queen three days to guess his name?

6. Why did Rumpelstiltskin return to the village?

7. How did the villagers feel when they saw Rumpelstiltskin returning?

8. Should Rumpelstiltskin have forgiven the villagers so easily?

General Questions

1. How does exclusion change people and the community?

2. Can you judge a person fairly by how they look?

3. Should a friend expect you to do things for them even if you don't want to?

4. Why is forgiveness important?

Research

What are illuminated manuscripts?

Thank you for taking time to read *Rumpelstiltskin's Child*. If you enjoyed it, please consider telling your friends or posting a short review. Word of mouth is an author's best friend and much appreciated. You can also vote for it on Goodreads listopia.

Website - http://www.BonnieFerrante.ca

Amazon - http://www.amazon.com/Bonnie-Ferrante/e/B007P7LFYG/ref=sr_ntt_srch_lnk_2?qid=1382025411&sr=8-2

facebook - Bonnie Ferrante - Author https://www.facebook.com/FerranteAuthor
            - Bonnie Ferrante - Books for Children
https://www.facebook.com/FerranteBooksForChildren

twitter - @BonnieFerrante

My Blog - http://bferrante.wordpress.com/

linkedin - http://www.linkedin.com/pub/bonnie-ferrante-tittaferrante/57/230/891

Goodreads - https://www.goodreads.com/author/show/4890077.Bonnie_Ferrante

Pinterest - http://www.pinterest.com/bferrante0365/boards/

Youtube - http://www.youtube.com/user/Bonnie0904

More Books by Bonnie Ferrante

Young Adult

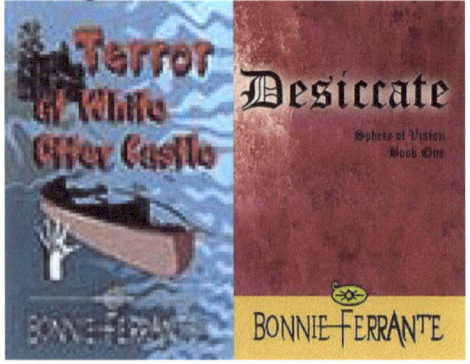

www.ingramcontent.com/pod-product-compliance
Lightning Source LLC
Chambersburg PA
CBHW041000170626
46815CB00002B/90

* 9 7 8 1 9 2 8 0 6 4 1 2 1 *